The Bygones

The Bygones

small
stories

by

Jim
Gibson

TANGERINE PRESS • LONDON • 2022

ISBN 978-1-910691-68-7 (paperback)
      978-1-910691-69-4 (hardback)

THE BYGONES. COPYRIGHT © 2022 JIM GIBSON
THIS EDITION FIRST PUBLISHED 2022 BY TANGERINE PRESS
UNIT 18
RIVERSIDE ROAD
GARRATT BUSINESS PARK
LONDON
SW17 0BA
ENGLAND
thetangerinepress.com

Tangerine Press books are printed on acid-free paper

Acknowledgements

Grateful acknowledgement is due to the editors of the publications and websites where the following stories first appeared: 'Jungle Banshee' in *3am Magazine*; 'Jamie on the Burger Van' in The Common Breath's online Fiction Series; 'You' in *Low Light*; 'A Bacon Sandwich' in the Burning House Press online Fiction Series; 'Miss Fitzgerald' in *Glove*. 'The Squirrel' was first published in the limited edition chapbook *The Hidden Valley* (HiVis Press, 2020); 'Gnomes' and 'Witch Play' were first published in the limited edition chapbook *Three Stories* (Tangerine Press/Sick Fly Publications, 2018).

The author and publisher also wish to extend their gratitude to Julia Soboleva, whose specially commissioned artwork can be found in the limited editions of this book.

Table of Contents

'In the midlands, there is a distinct architecture of folklore that is probably more grand than elsewhere in these lands. It is a vibrant cacophony of intertwining deities, mythical men and women, ghosts, demons and bygone friends of the forest. It is my prediction that we are still to see all of the evidence and will never fully understand to what extent the realms are passed between in this area. It seems that it has locally been accepted that there is magic in these peoples' mundanity and it goes unquestioned and therefore becomes hard to distinguish from time to time. It has been noted in texts that this part of England refused to kill its witches and has long since been seen as a threat, many links can therefore be drawn to the underfunding and lack of industry and development within the region, due to the level of magic still left there after the Christian invasion and the 'purification' of the British Isles. The only contemporary comparison is Ireland, where there are individuals with 'cures' for very specific illnesses, this being only one example of the magic that remains in that specific area. Here, however, the magic is not under any form of control and is only seen in certain situations and, even then, makes it hard for the people that witness it to believe as they have been subdued to a placid state like that of the rest of the country. Only, there is magic there . . .'

—*The Lost History of the East Midlands, 1868*
Graham Sterne

This book was banned a week after its release and only a few isolated copies remain

The Bygones

The Devil

When I met the Devil I was twelve years old. I'd started holding hands with Holly from the top end of the village and, even though I thought she was only messing me around when she said that she'd be my girlfriend, I still went along with it. That's something else about this time of my life (the bit about Holly, I mean) but I'd say you probably want to hear about the Devil, don't you? That's what you're here for, isn't it? First off, the devil was a he, I mean, it'd be pretty hard to tell on first glance. If you didn't have my insight, that is. They say that the Devil is inside all of us and that's probably true as a metaphor or whatever but I'm talking a real eight foot tall Devil beast that lets off a snarl but can talk and its flesh is red from heat with, like, a human torso but everything else animal: legs, hooves, HEAD and all.

It was after Christmas, the first time that I went to kiss Holly, the first time I'd ever gone in for a kiss and she had this snowball in her hand that I hadn't seen and, as I moved in, she slammed it in my face and rubbed it in and laughed. My face was red from the cold but burned and was hot and I think she felt bad cos she let me kiss her after that. I'll always remember those rosy cheeks and curly orange hair and her round, plump face. I thought she was so pretty. We stayed out in the dark, kissing on the step at the back of the welfare. I'd decided she wasn't messing me around at this point and I thought I'd stick with her forever, probably.

That wasn't the night I met the Devil though. That was a few weeks later. I was still with Holly. We were going strong. Still kissing. I even had her up in my room and we did a lot of lying down and kissing. This day though, I think I'd been at hers. Yeah, I remember, her dad had walked in on us and said I could stay but he wanted us downstairs so we went down and watched *Gone in 60 Seconds* with him. It was pretty good to be fair but when it was done he was sharper with the kicking out than I'd expected, a really direct *Right, out now, kid*. That was it. I mean, I'm not soft but I was a bit like, *Alright, pal, let the credits start.* I told you she lived up the top end of the village: near the woods. That's where you see the beasts and ghosts, right? Yep. But not this time. I walked home and could see my breath, down the hill where the frost really gets slippy. It got inch-thick with ice some years. We used to run and slide on our bellies as far as we could. That was before I started kissing with Holly, obviously. The old people would shout at us but we weren't bothered.

The light was on downstairs when I got back to my house and there was a white van outside with the engine running. I looked through the passenger side window and there he was. The Devil. Sitting at the wheel, holding it tight and sort of vibrating. You could tell he was red even in the poor light from the street. It was one of those moments where you look around for someone to show it to. Before I could take it all in, he turned and looked at me and I ran off. One of those head down runs that gets you where you're going quicker. I darted down the path and into my house. Mum was in the kitchen sewing like a stereotype but she hated sewing and would do anything to get out of it so make of that what you want. I'd not calmed down and shouted, *Mum! Mum! The Devil is sat in that van! Look Mum! It's a monster! Look! Look!* She looked out of the window from behind the curtain and tutted, speaking more to herself than to me, *Hasn't he bloody gone yet? You know him? It's Steve, yer uncle, he needs somewhere to stay but he's . . . oh, I dunno. I just don't want him to be around you.* I know what you're thinking and that's why I said: *Why does he look like that?* You know, to find out if I'd actually seen it right. *He's a weirdo. Can I go and talk to him? Why?* I shrugged, *Well, if he's my uncle. Go on then. You tell him I said he's gotta move as well; he can't stay there all night or I'll not hear the end of it.* She was always thinking of the neighbours, my mum.

I was a bit wary about it at first but I was the curious kind so didn't stop. Things needed investigating; like kissing. He was looking straight out front when I knocked on the passenger window. He leant over and wound the window down. *Uncle Steve?* His head twitched like Tourette's and there was a gargling in his throat. He took a deep breath. Stopped. Lit a fag. And turned to me. *You Kate's lad, John?* I got straight to it and asked, *Are you the Devil?* He laughed, *Take what work I can get nowadays. But, yeah. Here.* He got out of the van, his hooves hissing with each step on the ice as he walked round to the back. I thought he was going to show me a mattress where he slept or something but when he undid the padlock and opened the door, there was this gaping fiery hole. I could feel the heat really burning and he was looking at me with a little smile and he flicked his fag in. *Well? Is that Hell? No tricking you, is there, pal? You wanna see what's down there?* I shook my head. Not a chance. *Mum ses you've gotta move the van.* He nodded. *I know. I'm sick of sleeping down there, pal. There's nothing worse.* If you'd seen his face, you'd know he wasn't joking when he said there's nothing worse. Anyway, he drove off soon after that. My mum said, *Good riddance* and I never saw the Devil again. I wish I had, really, he seemed alright. No-one believed me when I told them about him, even Holly. My mum told me to forget about it.

Ah, I dunno . . . Shall I tell you? Well, I'm not proud of it but when I said I never saw him again, it wasn't EXACTLY true. There was this one day that me and my mates were out. They'd actually started to do this thing where they'd call round Holly's house for me because they knew I'd be there and once they'd got you then you had to go out, really. Holly would come sometimes but mostly I'd go on my own and she'd get grumpy cos that's what happens when you aren't in the honeymoon phase anymore, that's what my mum told me. Well, Holly didn't come out this day. It had stayed cold and the snow had turned to a slush in the places where it still hung around and we were just sorta traipsing round. I remember we found a wheelbarrow and Johnny pinched some lighter fluid from his dad and we filled it with bits of wood and stuff and lit it and walked up and down the street with this flaming ritual of youth. We thought it was the funniest thing. This burning wheelbarrow. But it was when we got down to the bottom car park that I noticed the van sitting there with the engine running. I told them that's the van my uncle, the Devil, lives in and they fell about laughing like they did the first time I told them. They said, *Your uncle lives in a van and thinks he's the Devil, righto! He's a homeless nutter, that's what I think!* I said, *Come on, I'll show.*

He was there with one of his little horns resting on the window of the passenger side, his legs up on the dash and you could clearly see his hooves. *Look!* They weren't though, they all had snowballs of slushy ice and started throwing them at the van and one even cracked the wing mirror. They didn't notice how quickly the snowballs melted on the back end, where the gateway to Hell was, and when my uncle woke up, he ran to get out like it was a battlefield outside. And do you know what I did? The hero of your story. What I did was, I pulled my scarf up over my nose so he didn't recognise me. Then, you know what I did? I picked up the slushy snow and started pelting him too. It was funny how he kept slipping when we hit him but I couldn't help feeling bad, if I'm honest. We legged it after that and when we stopped for breath, I said *I told you he was the Devil.* One of them told me that if every uncle is what they dress up as then his uncle was Ozzy Osborne. Everyone laughed, but I didn't. They missed the hooves and everything. After that, if they brought it up I joined in and called him a freak as well. That was honestly the last time I saw him. I swear this time.

It was around spring when I decided I'd had enough of Holly. It was getting a bit boring and the sun was starting to get warmer. I decided to not text her back or anything and managed to avoid her for a good couple of months. When she happened to walk by one day I was nervous but she totally ignored me. It was a bad move on my end and I do feel really guilty about it but it seemed like a good idea at the time.

Jungle Banshee

It was called home and I lived there and I didn't really go out much. I'd go to the shop in the morning and buy cans of energy drinks and take them home to sit on my X-Box, breaking only for oven chips and oven fish and to feel bad when I looked at the mess of an oven. I could ignore the rest of the house, with screen eyes you can do things while still having the game running behind the surface so that the scum in the toilet could be ignored, the dust, the food splattered walls, all of that. Apart from the oven: thick with grot and whenever you opened it to get your food, the room would flood with smoke. I'd long ago taken the battery out of the fire alarm to stop that fucker going off whenever I made anything. And then it was back up to my room, to my games.

I don't get depressed at home, I get depressed when I have to leave; when I have to sign on or when I have to visit people. I mean, I don't visit people that often but I do have to go to the Job Centre a bit and it's a ball ache. A waste of time. Me going all the way up there for them to keep me waiting. If I'm ever late, that's it: SANCTIONED. If they're late then that's fine. And, you see people in there being like teachers' pets, asking about jobs or if they can get onto courses and bragging to their advisors about interviews they'd been to.

On this day, I walked back from the Job Centre instead of getting the bus to save a bit of money. They'd pointed out a few jobs for me to apply for when I got home and I said I would and they looked me up and down and asked *Have you got any nice clothes for an interview?* Since I put all the weight on, I haven't bought any proper clothes like jeans or anything, I just have this one pair of navy blue trackies and a few baggy t-shirts with, like, No Fear or Lonsdale on them so I said *Yeah, course I have* and they waved me off. But, walking home,

I was really down. Looking at everything going past me, cars, birds, people, buildings, they all seemed to have a purpose and I was panting with a bag full of Monster and an open can in my hand and got to looking at the ground all the way home, the rough tarmac and pavement potholes, the litter everywhere, the fly tipping on street corners where people live. It wasn't just my house that was like this, it was the whole town. As people went to and from work they must have had screen eyes too but filled with jobs and work and they couldn't see it all. It was a fucking state. I crushed the can and dropped it down to join a condom, a needle and a nappy. No-one would notice.

When I got home it was dark inside so I opened the blinds that lit the dust particles in the air and saw the X-Box, then I saw the rest of the room and decided it was time for a clean-up. Head, house and soul. I gave the whole place as deep a clean as I could and it took hours but I was pretty happy with it when I'd finished and I sat on the settee with a chip sandwich and looked around. It seemed bigger but it was still quiet. I turned on my laptop and and after a while found this live, sorta, radio channel that played song after song of this almost lift music with like calm rapping and stuff. The music was weird but they also had, like, Simpsons videos behind them, only all purple and like it was played on an old scratched VHS. I looked to the top right and there was a little box where people could talk and they were all being really friendly and giving advice and stuff so I typed a few words, my heart racing from the caffeine and the worry. It had my gamer tag, JungleBanshee111, and I wanted to delete what I'd written as soon as I had written it but there was no way to. Then the responses came, THAT'S SHITTY JUNGLEBANSHEE, I KNOW THE FEELING and NO WORRIES, YOU'RE WITH FRIENDS HERE. I don't know why but it was comforting. I chatted with them about all sorts while the music played all nice and soothing in the background, I sorta forgot it was even playing. Everyone on here had their own problems and I was just one of many. I went on it more and more over the next few days and kept the house tidy. I'd got my gaming down to a couple of hours a day and I wasn't even really trying, to tell you the truth, I only wanted to listen to this strange music and talk to some people. It was probably about a week in when I realised it. Someone asked everyone how they get through school cos they were finding it really hard. Then, when people replied, it turned out that they were all 13 or 14. I'd been talking to children and it never once crossed my mind that they could be so young. Then they asked: HOW OLD ARE YOU JUNGLE? I was the only one that hadn't answered and under the pressure I put: 14. I mean, I knew I shouldn't've but it was the first time I wasn't lonely in so long, so the 14 idea seemed to keep my options open for a little bit longer. And, I knew I shouldn't but I kept talking to them. I thought back about my time at school and said it as if it was happening now, it was like I wasn't lying, just getting the tenses wrong. No-one was harming anyone. But when I went to bed each night it wasn't as satisfying as it was before I knew I was talking to kids. Commenting on their dreams. I had to stop.

I was surprised when I got an email saying that I'd got an interview for a job that I'd applied for. It was only picking and packing at a warehouse but for some reason, I felt really good about it. I headed up to the Job Centre and told my advisor that I needed some clothes for an interview and he smiled, saying *I thought you had smart clothes?* For the first time I was straight up with him, *None that fit me anymore.* He gave me a voucher for Matalan and I got a suit and everything.

The interview was basic, one fella in a room telling me it was informal and not to be nervous and my suit chafed and he smiled and asked me about myself and I said *What do you mean?* And he said *You know, I want to find out a bit about YOU.* It was daft but straight away I thought of JungleBanshee. I shrugged my shoulders, *I'm into gaming, I like spending time with family.* Then, I dunno, I just turned into someone else again, *Actually, I'm really into finding out how things work, I like to communicate with people, I think that I'm good at . . .*

I went on and on and I'd never heard myself be like this. I walked out the door feeling like a new person. A smile was on my face. A genuine smile and a proper joy.

At home it was different. I put the kettle on and rang my mum. She didn't believe it. After a week I still hadn't heard anything back so I decided, fuck it, I'll ring them. So I did. I asked for the fella that had seen me and they put him on and he said that he was sorry but they chose someone else for the job.

That was it.

Back

floating

in empty

space.

The house was big again. I put the radio station back on and they cheered to see me back online. I made up some shit about having not been chosen for the school play and made up an aunt dying and they all gave me their wishes. Five days later I headed to the oven with screen eyes and tripped on the boxes on the floor. I fell to the ground and was stuck staring at a ketchup stain on the wall. It had little bits of mould sprouting from it. It was hard to get up so I just laid there for a bit and listened to my own heavy breath.

Jamie on the Burger Van

There's no-one else to talk to so I might as well make the most of it. It's a horrible thought but I can't help thinking that his life is sort of like an animal's, you know? Like he sort of doesn't know he's here and if he died tomorrow, he could still come down the next day and talk to me exactly the same as he does every day. I hand him a coffee. That's why he comes back. For the free coffee. And to tell me the same stories he always does. About how he got to actually ride in an Eddie Stobart lorry once and how they're having a party for his birthday at the home he lives in and how he knows one of the market traders sells dirty DVDs but you have to ask him for them. He points the stall out to me and I stand up to see where he means. I'm higher than him in the van. The stall is empty, like a lot of them are now, and I wonder if he sees time the same way as me. I wonder if he sees the past in that empty stall. As he turns I see the big scar that travels down the back of his head like a map of a route down a mountain, with bulges on either side of it. I've never asked him what happened and never will. He sometimes calls me by a name that's not mine and I assume it's the name of whoever had a van parked up here a long time before me but there's no way of telling.

The man from the e-cig stall comes over. He's one to watch out for. Last time he hid a cock pump on the woman's stall who sells curtains and that netting stuff that goes in the window. I'm sure her stock was all white when she first had it out but now it looks reclaimed from a heavy smoker's house whose lungs finally gave way. It was quite funny when he did it though, hid the cock pump, he kept looking over to me, smiling and winking when the old people were looking around. That's all you get on the market, really: old people. I get a few younger ones on their lunch breaks and the e-cig man does too, but apart from that it's mostly old people. Anyway, when it happened I saw this old lady hold it up and ask what it was. The e-cig man was in stitches so it was obvious who'd put it there but he didn't care. I don't think either the woman on the stall or the old lady worked out what it was but he enjoyed it anyway. He asks me how trade is going and I tell him *Same as usual: shit. What about you?* He says he's not doing bad but I know it's not true cos I've only seen about two people go up all day. Town's littered with e-cig shops now anyway, they're nearly on par with charity shops. He slides some coins onto the counter and I chuck a burger on the griddle. It's only enough for a cheese burger but I always stick a few bits of bacon on.

He asks me if I've heard *ote of him who used ta stand over there*, and nods his head to the empty spot next to me. There used to be a jacket potato van with a funny little man running it who only ever wore a black shirt and trousers, had slicked back hair and a chain around his neck with a cross on it. He always used to tell stories and drink red wine from a polystyrene cup; stories about how it used to be. I remember him from way back when I was at school and we'd sneak out at dinnertime to get a cheap spud from him for a quid. Anyway, he's not allowed back now for cutting someone's hand with a knife. The fella was kicking off about not getting enough cheese and reached over to grab some more. A big chap in a vest and shorts with tribal tattoos up his neck. One of the steroid kinds. The spud man didn't seem to care; he slashed his hand and blood pissed out everywhere. I had to grab my first aid kit and bandage him up cos the spud man sort of saw it as 'problem solved'. I remember being surprised that the big youth didn't do more to kick off, I'm guessing there must have been more truth in the spud man's big tales than I'd gave him credit for. I cob-up the burger and bacon and pass it over, saying *No mate, not a word.* He snorts a laugh: *Fuckin nut job* and walks back off to his stall.

I know it's not going to last, sitting out here but it's turned into more of an obsession than a living. It's like I'm present at the collapse of something that no-one cares about. There's a few fancy new stalls that come from time to time, you know, artisan bread and, like, trays of olives, but they never seem to stick it for more than a few weeks. A bit like I should have done; gone to find a busy lay-by or summet. The only time I've seen it really busy in ages was when there were people raising money for the funeral of a young lad who'd been knocked off his motorbike by a white van. The whole of town was out to buy some stuff and support it and they'd sold out of the raffle tickets by twelve which is unheard of. Everyone knew that the lad was a right sort but you can't say that when they're dead, can you? The veg lady told me how she felt sorry for the van driver and I looked at her with a question mark and she told me that it wasn't his fault. The lad was one of these who drive around the estate at silly speeds doing wheelies and that he went straight over the give way bit when the van went into him and killed him. She said the van driver beat himself up about it and was getting threats left, right and centre. It sounded like he'd got a shit deal but it's safer not to choose a side on stuff like this.

The man with the scar hasn't said a word for a long while but still stands in front of me. He's facing away and sipping the coffee that looks far too hot to drink. He turns and looks straight at me with those deep eyes and I get the feeling that, if he was to not come down one day, then I'd disappear like the stall that sits empty. Like I'm only here in his memory. He blinks and doesn't say a word and I can feel the atoms in my body shudder. He puts his drink onto the counter and walks away and for some reason I know that he isn't going to come back again. I look out the open back door of the van, past the generator that vibrates and hums, into the graveyard of the church that's directly behind me. There's a statue of an angel holding a baby in amongst the overgrown and fading gravestones. Her face has been worn away and Her arms are chipped.

It's nothing that a burger and a weak cup of tea can fix.

The Squirrel

We used to feed this squirrel when we were children. I forget the name of it, Rodger or Sirrel or something like that. We'd bring it Kit Kats and it would sit with a single chocolate finger in both its hands (or paws or mitts or whatever), gnawing away quickly like a cartoon character. Me and my sister thought it was amazing how it'd come and have a picnic with you and we'd talk to it on the benches where we learnt not to try and stroke it cos then it'd run away. The only person that could touch it was my granny. He'd even sometimes go and sit up on her shoulder and she went about her business as usual with a grey squirrel sat up there, occasionally passing it bits of nuts and things when she came across them in her bag. We used to joke about her being a woodland pirate and, well, she was a bit; the same way that pirates live their lives mainly at sea, she was always in the woods, walking the dogs and enjoying the peace of it all I suppose. That's what she was trying to do with me and my sister: give us a taster of nature so that we know it's there, so that we know that we can always come back to it should we need to.

I always loved nature from then on. There was no need to return to it because I never left it: a teenager foraging in the woods with my pocket sized edition of some book that shows the different kinds of mushrooms. I'd tick off what I found and put all of the different edible ones into separate sandwich bags. Blueys were the easiest to find and you could make a bob or two on them; all the old people would happily pay a quid for a bag of blueys, *Ohhh*, they'd say, *nowt beats the taste of a bluey to tek yer back*. Some of them I didn't fancy though, like jelly ears. My sister, on the other hand, had lost her way about the woods. I once took her in, telling her I had a shortcut to the bus stop on the main road where the quicker busses stop (the ones that don't do all of the estates) but really I was checking if there was anything of that 'nature-awe' left in her. When we walked in, she looked around herself but I could see that she had some sort of barrier that stopped her from really taking anything in. She didn't care one bit for it and turned back pretty soon, saying how she'd rather wait for the long bus *cos it's fucking gross in here. Look at the mud on me boots!* She had too many things whirling through her head to be interested in something so still on the surface.

I carried on anyway. She told me later that, when she got out, there were all police cars pulling up with their lights on and they wrapped their tape from tree to tree to stop people from entering. She said they wouldn't let her go back and find me: a likely story. But I kept going, never having known danger in the woods at fourteen. I saw some black tarp and went to investigate. There was a man underneath in a sleeping bag. He had wild hair with twigs sticking out of it and a grey beard and he opened his eyes when I was right over him and looking straight down. He unzipped his bag and as he threw a leg out he laughed and said, *What the fuck do you want, lad? Nothing,* I shrugged, *I was just seeing what was over here. What's that in yer pocket?* I pulled out the blueys and my mushroom book and told him what they were. *Let's see this little book you've got then.* As he flicked through it, I sat on a rock and started asking him questions about how it was to live out here, it never crossed my mind to ask why, but he didn't answer. He just kept flicking through and squinting. Then finally: *This one, this one here.* He passed me the book. *It doesn't say anything but they're the ones you want to be picking, cook them up for the old people you sell em to; give em a right good trip. HAH!* I circled the one he pointed out and wrote the name he called them next to the picture: liberty caps. I thanked him and offered him a Kit Kat that I had in my pocket. He was reluctant at first but took it eventually. I could see in his eyes that he wanted it really and, as he snapped one of the fingers off, I said see ya later and carried on my journey.

At the other end I met the blockade of coppers who told me about the *dangerous criminal at large* who they had reason to believe was hiding out in the woods. They asked me if I'd seen anything and shook my head, *Not unless you're after a squirrel.* I wasn't going to be a grass, we should all be able to hide in the silence if we want to.

You

A mouse came into the room. It stopped. Turned. Left. The room seemed empty. Still. Forgotten. But there was someone in there. Someone sat in the corner. It was you. You were stuck. Not moving. Broken. The dust had gathered everywhere apart from the path that led from your seat to the back door. Not the front door. The back door was bliss. Even in the rain it always felt sunny at the back door. And the air. The outside air. The air that flew around your body like life. But not the front door. No. Not anymore. But you hadn't been to the back door today and it had got dark. The dark used to be great. The bat that circled the garden, the owls that were heard in the distance. Now it's usually silent. The odd weekend party heard over the fence or a neighbour's row but not enough to write home about. You just couldn't enjoy the dark too much anymore. Or the artificial light. The blinding dullness of a bulb lit in the middle of the room made it look vulgar. You just got to sitting at this point. Sitting and thinking. Thinking back. Back to when you were a part of the community. And you were, whether you wanted to be or not; you grew up here and were a part of the community but then something happened. Was it inside of you or outside of them? Who knows? But you didn't want to be a part of this community any longer and it left you vulnerable, didn't it? You thought it meant that you were stronger but it didn't. You forced all of the memories down as much as you could but they kept floating up. Floating as tears or awkward laughter and who knows what's real with memories, anyway? They're all you had but they don't feel real because you couldn't touch them.

You saw someone walk past the window. You knew them so there's no need to describe them. There's a memory with them in it. It goes something along the lines of when your dad bought that new dog home and she was desperate to come and see the puppy and so you let her into your house where you sat on your knees in the kitchen laughing when it licked your faces and ended up knocking you over. No. That's not right. It was a cat and you laughed when it climbed the curtains. Or did she cry when it attacked her in a panic and ran away and you soothed the cat and comforted it and told it that it'd be alright. Or was it a baby? That's the problem. And you were sure she looked in the window when she passed. Did she wonder if you were dead? Maybe you could have asked her about this memory, see what really happened. That'd be the day. You decided it was time for a brew and remembered the mound of cups on the side so decided not to move. Is this what death feels like? You'd seen death a few times. You were certain of that one. It lived in the walls of the house, in the damp that rose and the cracks that fell. The house was death. It was your uncle's face after the car accident, your dad's lungs after the cancer, your grandad's mind when the dementia had fully set in, it was your baby's screams for the two nights you had it home: too busy and worried to name it before it died. Kevin. That's what you'd both called him afterwards. He was lovely. Even you and them, the twelve years of you and them, was hard to picture by this point. Laughs, fights, highs and lows all bundled into one ball of twelve years that could have been picked apart but it seemed like too much work. And pointless. It would only make you wonder and you know what wonder leads to.

It had been dark for weeks. You pulled at the blinds every few hours to see if the sun had come out to go into the garden but it hadn't. It was hard staying still for so long. Your muscles would cramp up to check you were still there. You could feel your face melting away. You felt like you'd soon be a puddle on the floor. You thought about how, when you did melt, you'd seep into the carpet and be forgotten. A stain for someone else to deal with. You wondered if there was any news about when the sun would be out again but that was all it was. A wonder. Can you remember the time you were at that family party at the welfare and you kissed the fittest person in the room and your cousins were jealous? That was when you first met them, wasn't it? Or were you too shy to talk to them and they gave you their number on the way out? Or had you been alone all along? There was no sign that they were ever here and this was your family home, it always had been. You felt like you moved sometimes but only because of the wind. And you heard voices, you're sure you heard voices that you know but stayed still. It was safer to stay still and wait for it to get light outside. It would get light eventually, you were sure of it.

A Bacon Sandwich

I leave the house in my jogging bottoms and hoody. It's the not so early morning in spring and I'm headed up to the corner shop for a loaf of bread and bacon, you know the stuff that says with added water on the packet like it's something to be proud of, because it's Saturday and when you live on your own you've got to give yourself little rewards for making it to another weekend. Couples get to lie in together with hangovers but when you're on your own the bed doesn't stay warm and a bacon sandwich on buttered white bread is a home remedy that feels like it's been unconsciously passed down through the ages.

My neighbour's already outside, sweeping up the mess. She's composed when she apologises about last night and I quickly tell her that it's alright and lie to her that I didn't even hear anything, was there a scene, what scene? She's a nice lady and I don't want to hurt her feelings but I saw the whole thing. She'd had her fella round again, one of those sorts who everyone knows isn't made for a relationship but who somehow always seems to have a girlfriend. He came round drunk and I don't know the ins and outs of it all but from the screams I worked out that he'd been accusing her of sleeping around. After a while of crashing and bashing, she took it out to the street where she hurled pots from the garden that shattered on the road when they missed and made a dull thud when they hit him. One skimmed past his head and put a big dent in the passenger door of his car. He got in, wound down the window, shouted his last dues about her being crazy and drove off with an angry, drunken skid.

I was watching by this time and convinced myself that I was only doing it in case he hit her. My adrenaline was pumping thinking about it. There was nothing I wanted less than to intervene but my thumping heart was preparing me for the occasion. She'd been knocked about by another bad egg before, I heard it through the walls and, because it took me by surprise, I didn't do anything. I didn't dare move in case she could tell that I was there, not doing anything. It was a night of shame. This time I was ready with a lump hammer in my hand but, as I said, he took the pots that were flung at him and headed off. Then I watched her cry on the street. I hadn't expected this while I stood there pumped up for a battle that I knew I couldn't handle. How could a man with a lump hammer and a beating heart full of adrenaline ever go and comfort someone? Again, I was unprepared. So I hid.

Walking back from the shop, I saw she was emptying her dustpan into the bin. I asked her if she wanted a bacon sandwich and smiled. She nodded and said yeah, alright, bring it round and I'll get the teas on. I cooked it so it was nice and crispy and brought it round to hers with a bottle of red and a bottle of brown to not make assumptions. We sat on her garden in the cool air with soft bacon sandwiches and piping tea while her rabbit hopped about, exploring the bushes. She didn't want sauce, said she just liked to taste the bacon.

Miss Fitzgerald

Well I was outside work, having a fag, yer know how the front leads onto the high street? Well I was out there, under a bit of shelter I'd found and there weren't many people out cos of the weather and I'm sure it was maybe cos of the shape of me hood but I could hear everyone's conversations crisp and clear. Must've sucked it all in or summet. The one that stood out to me was these two young girls. Lovely looking but you'd've thought that they were a bit young if it weren't for the tattoos up their legs and that; they must've got caught out in the rain or summet but they din't really seem to care. One of em was pushing a pram and I heard her say to the other one that she'd rather her fella came outta jail first and then if it's not working two months down the line, it's not working, but at least they gave it a proper go, ya know. I liked her thinking and it struck me that she was a good soul, ya know, got her head screwed on for the important things. To have a girl like that, he must be a good sort, ya know, treats women right an all that. I was a bit jealous that I couldn't find a bird like that. But that were it. It stuck with me but I din't think that I'd ever hear owt about it again.

It was a coupler week later when I was at a bit of a party at a house not far from yours, just up the hill, round the back of the cemetery. Church Lane, is it? Ahr, it don't matter anyway, but it was one of the twins we used to go to school with, I forget which, was throwing the party but I thought it was going to be one of them free-for-alls that've got a bit rarer now we're over 28; it really wasn't. It was more civilised than they used to be but I din't really mind cos I wan't really feeling much like going mad anyway. You know what it's like when you see all them lot from school that you never liked anyway, and they're all talking about their nice lives in their new build houses and all that and I thought of the one bed flat with empty pizza boxes and its mysterious smell and how I came from there this evening and would go back alone. I only went cos I thought you were coming, but ya never did so I did summet that I probably shouldn't've done as a mature adult but they were all getting on me nerves that much, so I went to the kitchen and filled my backpack with all of the booze I could and, you're gonna laugh at this. I'd brought this acid. Cos I thought YOU were gonna be there, and, ya know, it were gonna be a PARTY. And I know it were a waste of money but I dropped all of the tabs into the only two wine bottles that I left em then I did one out of the back door. They'd be on me for nicking the cans and with the acid and that but I couldn't be doing with even saying bye and getting away elegantly so I slipped out the back door like a suspicious bastard and made for home.

It was round on Farley's Lane when I saw her. She was outside Jack's with her kid in the pram and another kid, a bit older, still in his school polo, trying to do kick-ups but only managing a few each time. She was at the bottom of that great massive set of steps that's outside of the shops, up to the main road, and I was at the top looking down. The older kid was still too young to help her so she turned her back to me and started juddering the pram up backwards, one step at a time. It must've riled the kid up a bit cos it started screaming so I raced down like the hero that I am and offered her some help. She smiled at me and I grabbed the bottom of the pram and carried it with her, all the way to the top, without even a word between us. She thanked me at the top and turned to leave. It all seemed natural and I asked her where she was going. She said Home and I told her how nice a night it was and that I've got some wine and some cans if she wanted to take the kids down to the field for a bit of a kick around and chill out and that. I knew I'd overstepped the mark after I said it but, still, I waited for a reply, ya know.

That was it. Next thing I know, we were down on the bottom field. She was chugging on a bottle of Echo Falls rosé and I cracked a can of Stella. It was bliss. Me and the lad got on like a house on fire, playing cross bar challenge and stuff. He was better than me but I pretended to her I was letting him win. The little girl too, she was adorable; I didn't think I really liked babies but this one, she laughed whenever she saw me. Her little dimples in her cheeks made my heart lift. But her, Danielle Fitzgerald, that's her name. She's got long dark hair and a high pitched laugh. We were so kicking it off. I'd say those, like, silly little jokes that you say in a relationship, you know, the kind that no-one really finds funny, and she'd really give em a high-pitched belly laugh. It was a great night, I'm glad you weren't at the party. I sorta . . . sorta felt . . . I dunno: useful. Wanted. Like I was in the world again, not just observing it.

It wasn't till she invited me back to hers that I thought about the fella in prison. Thought about him walking through the door and catching me with his woman but I let these thoughts rise and fade, it was too good to stop it all now, for all that. After she'd told me about her job at Heron, the night classes at the local college in, like, nail art and massage and all that, after all that, she brought up her fella. He wasn't the father to the kids. The kids' dad had gone off straight after the second one was born and she didn't even know where he was but she was glad cos he used to bash her about and everything. She didn't want the second kid but she was stuck with him she told me, she even told me how he bashed her in while she was pregnant; that the baby was really premature and they didn't think she'd pull through but she did. Her fella came on the scene and chased him off, and good job too. He'd moved in with her and got caught out cos he was growing weed in the flat that he'd got off of the social. She said she'd been round a few times and it was like a jungle. You come out feeling dizzy just from the fumes. Can you imagine? We'd be in our element there but it's shitty that he got banged up. He tells her that he shouldn't be with her when he gets out cos what would other people say when she's trying her best and he's been inside for having a grow on? She said he was probably right but I could see her eyes sort of droop when she said it. I got up then and grabbed my things without saying anything. I think she knew what was happening too because she never said a word either. I wanted to stay so bad. I looked at the baby in the cot by her feet, the young lad with his head on her lap, fast on, and Danielle sat under the floor lamp with that glass of rosé, soft lit and tender. I smiled when I opened the door and said for her to call me if it didn't work out with him. My heart had opened for the evening. It was a family waiting for a *me*, but it turned out they already had one.

I walked back to my flat and went straight to bed alone; I'd nearly broken this bad habit tonight but not quite. I scrolled on my phone in the darkness and laughed as I read the posts from the people at the party. Fuckin maggots.

The Artist

In not so many words, he told me about the man that he saw around the bins at the back of his flat; the new flat he'd got, the one above the card shop in town. He said it was when he saw the man between his car and his neighbour's that he went downstairs to check it out. Yer know, this man looked dirty. Untrustworthy. At least that's what I made of what he told me. He thought he was gonna put his fist through the window, I think that was what he said, or summet like that, I dunno. All I know is that; he thought he was up to no good. When he got down to the bottom, he stopped. He saw the man picking up cans, yer see, he had white plastic bags full of em. I knew the back of that flat from long before my mate moved in there; people had been using that place to fly tip for years. Drop off any old crap there, one seater settees, mattresses, bedside tables, all sortsa shit scattered across the tarmac. I was a bit surprised that he had his car parked there to be honest. My mate told me how they'd all agreed to having this feral cat that they take it in turns to feed, to keep the rats away but even that fucked off after a bit. So, he said that he thought he'd leave this bloke with the cans for a bit, just to see, yer know, and went back upstairs to the top window. Said he watched him for quite a while. Watched him gathering up all these bits and bobs. When my friend told me this I nodded to him, *Scrap* I said, like I knew what I was on about. *Well . . . That's what I thought.* He went on, my mate, telling me this story about when he was on the streets that I'd heard a few times before and it ended with his usual: *I'd rather shoot someone and go to jail than be back out there. Prison is like Butlin's compared to that.* I don't know too much about prison but I'd say you've gotta have it bad for it to be like a holiday, yer know what I mean?

He said he left him to it. Poor sod. But when he came back later on, later that day, after he'd been out meeting some friends; he caught a glimpse of him in the bushes. All the ground was clear, he said. I mean, I assume the mattress and settee were still there, he never mentioned them, but all the crap on the floor had ended up in the bins and the place was all neatened out. He told me how the floor sorta looked sweaty, like it'd got all clammy underneath the boxes, the fast food wrappers, the nappies and everything. He said he nodded to the man as he walked past and noticed that he was using a penknife to hack away the branches on the bush. At this point it was half formed into a rugged dome. The man said hello and my friend walked back to the flat.

Once he'd told me all of this, I couldn't get it off of my mind. Everywhere I looked, I saw jobs that I thought this man could do. I don't know why I was hiring him in my head all of the time to neaten up places that weren't even mine to neaten, but that's what I did. Over the weeks I'd phone my mate up with new questions: why was he doing it and did he live in the flats, then moving on to how do you know someone isn't paying him? My friend made it clear that he didn't have any answers, that he was bored of the subject and that he wished he'd never even mentioned it. He laughed one of them sorta pissed off laughs and told me to forget about it.

It wasn't till today that he rang me. He told me that the fella had come back and that if I want answers, well, now's the time to come and find out for myself. So, that's what I did. I was still in my scruffs from painting the landing when I jumped on the 92 into town. I got off a few stops before the town bus station and panted as I darted through the gennels and jittys and up round the back of the flat. I saw him: yellow t-shirt, wild hair, a sort of Romanian tan and jeans with brown muck on the knees. He was a bit up from my friend's, pulling weeds out of the potholes and curb stones that supported them. I watched him. Then I watched him move onto one of those summer flower beds that gets taken away in winter and brought out in spring. He stuck his fingers deep into the muck and pulled the plants out, one by one, with the whole roots dangling like innards that shouldn't be exposed. Like my mate before, I was a bit taken aback and thought that foul play must be on the cards here. Why would he possibly be taking all of the plants out, yer know? I sat down, resting against red bricks and rolled a fag to not draw attention to myself. When all of the plants were out and scattered around him, the plant bed looked naked. I felt a frown as, one by one, he placed the plants back into the bed; taking a few step backs to see it as a whole, then moving forward again. It was miraculous when he finished. The bed wept with colour and brought to my stomach the feeling of seeing a coy child smile. It was uncanny.

He perched on the box and grabbed his tin of tobacco from his back pocket and I thought that this was my time to approach him. I walked over and he looked up when my feet were near him. *Alright.* That's what I said. *Alright*, was his reply.

I walked home like I'd seen a miracle. I kicked myself for not saying more but what would you say, anyway?

Little Robbie

Trevor ses his mum said that I can stop round his house tonight. I like it at Trevor's cos there's always people doing stuff: his brother, his mum, his dad, me and him. I've never stopped round anyone's house before. His mum tells me that she's going to go round to my house to check if it's OK with my mum. She knows my mum from when they were at school and stuff. When Trevor's mum goes out, his brother comes in the kitchen with his mate. They're pulling stuff from the fridge like milk and yoghurts and stuff and they roll them fags with weed in like my brother would. I tell them that I can roll them and Trevor tells them that I can't but I can cos I used to roll them for MY brother and they let me have a go. I show Trevor that I can and that shuts him up but he goes a bit grumpy and wants to go out. I tell him that I like hanging around with the older lads so we stay for a bit. They ignore us mostly but then Trevor's brother says that he shagged this girl and it was like 'fucking a bag of spanners' and it makes me laugh loads. Trevor doesn't laugh cos he doesn't get it. Trevor's brother and his mate look at me and ask what I know about shagging. I tell them that I've had sex before and they ask me what it feels like, so I put my finger on the inside of my mouth and say: *like that.* They laugh but then say that it's pretty true and I know I haven't had sex but I have touched one so I know that it's right, anyway.

Trevor's mum gets back and it's funny to see how his brother and his mate scramble to hide the weed and stuff and go out the back door before she gets in, leaving the milk out and these little yoghurt pots with spoons in. *My* brother wouldn't have been scared of *my* mum. Trevor's mum just huffs and tidies it all away while she tells me that it's alright with my mum that I stop over tonight and that she left me some money for school and hands me a five pound note. I know something's up cos Mum never has any money so I ask if she was up when she went round and Trevor's mum tells me that she was. I take the money and half an hour later I'm eating pasta with Trevor and his mum and dad and think about how it tastes weird. It's a good weird, though. I've had to eat dog food for the past few nights cos there wasn't anything else in the cupboards, not that I'd let anyone know. I always brush my teeth loads afterwards but there's no toothpaste at our house so it takes ages to get the taste out with just water. And then I think about the things that I can buy with my fiver from the corner shop in the morning so that I don't have to pinch sandwiches out of other people's lunchboxes. Trevor asks to speak to his mum in the hallway and his dad doesn't look up from his food when we hear Trevor telling his mum that he doesn't want me to stay over. I don't hear what his mum says back to him but I hear him moaning and when he comes back in he doesn't look at me either; his cheeks are red and he stares at his food and digs it with his fork.

Later that night, Trevor doesn't want to play on the PlayStation even though I tell him that, if we turn the sound off, no-one will even notice. I'm laid on my back with Trevor's feet in my face while he rolls around every two seconds. I like this house and stuff but I've got this feeling in my belly that means I want to go home. Even the ceiling looks like their ceiling. Other people's houses are weird.

I get my stuff together and I know Trevor's awake. He's turned to the wall to pretend that he doesn't notice me. He can be like this sometimes when his mum invites me round. I can hear the telly on downstairs and I go down anyway and quietly out the back door and around to the front, through the jitty. Two streets away is Nonnar's. Mum banned me from Nonnar's when they fell out a couple of years ago when I was eight but I still used to go round quite a bit but I don't anymore. She didn't even come round when our Dale died and Mum said that wasn't right. Dale was my brother and he was out on his bike and he went over the train lines when the barriers were down. Another kid from my school was there when it happened. He said that he wasn't supposed to tell me but there was pieces of Dale scattered all down the train track. He said he saw an arm just laying in the middle of the road.

I knock on Nonnar's door and I can see she's still up from the flickering colours in the window. She comes and opens up in her pyjamas and asks what I want, why I'm here, why I'm not at home, why that no-good mother of mine hasn't got me tucked up in bed. I tell Nonnar that Mum really needs her help, that she's got really bad and doesn't even go out anymore. Even to the shops. She ses that she'll have nothing more to do with her after she pinched that money from her and says that Mum'll have no kids left at this rate and that it'd probably be for the best. She huffs out air and tells me to come in and stop with her for a bit but I don't like how she talks about Mum. I'm the only one Mum's got left; it's just me and her now. I shout BITCH at her with this lump in my throat. I shout I HATE YOU and I run off back to our house: number 23 with the white step and boarded up top half of the window.

Inside, Mum's on the settee asleep, like I thought she would be, so I nudge her and tell her to look, that I've got a fiver for us to get something nice to eat but she doesn't wake up. I fold the fiver and slot it into her jeans pocket and I notice, on the table, right next to her face, there's a school photo of our Dale and a white cider bottle with only spit-back left.

In my room, Dale's half is exactly the same as he left it with pictures of rappers with bandanas around their faces and stuff. The only time I used to cross over was to feed his tarantula but even that's curled up and dead now. I see his old mp3 player and grab it along with the duvet off of Dale's bed for Mum. I chuck it over her and it looks warm so I get down to my pants and shiver while I slip in with her and curl right up into her belly. I press play on the mp3 player and there's loads of songs that I didn't expect him to like; slow songs like Snow Patrol and stuff. I like songs with sad words and I know that Mum does too so I put a headphone in her ear and one in mine and then I fall asleep.

Susan

There was always a chill in the air at this time of year but when she breathed tonight it was different. It made her not sure if she'd ever been up this early. There were small crystals in the air, when she breathed out it was a solid tunnel and when she breathed in it almost hurt. She had her hi-vis on and was walking down the hill to where she could see the stained corrugated roof that spread over all of the land that she called Work, to people who asked where she'd been.

There were a few outside already with plastic cups of steam and fags of smoke at the entrance. She saw the nub bin had filled up with water and the frozen nubs that had been floating on top were fossilised until there was some warmer weather. Her body hated her. The people said hello in varied accents and she said hello back, smiled through puffy eyes and headed for the vending machine. 20p for a coffee. White with two sugars. The first sip burnt her lips so she carried it to the canteen, pulled a chair off the stack and sat at a white table staring at the TV up on the wall that hadn't been turned on yet. She was always early. The bus times were difficult to work around. A few months ago she'd have been out there smoking with the rest of them but since the bump started showing, she decided to stop. For the baby's health, obviously, but also so that she didn't get people judging her. Oh God, how she'd kill for a fag in these cold mornings, though. Quarter to five and she hoped she hadn't left the heating on at home. She'd heard something on the radio about memories. It was about how, when you do different things or, like, more things, time seems to go quicker but afterwards it feels longer because you've created more memories and the opposite; when you do things you've done before or the same thing over and over, time seems to go slower but then afterwards, seems quicker because of the lack of memories. The past ten years or so have flown, she thought, as she stared at the blank screen, trying to work out what distorted image she could see in the reflection.

Some of them started to come in. They all pulled up chairs and sat together around a table. Their time was probably going quicker than hers. Time would go quick for her baby. Until it wasn't a baby and then it would seem like a blink of the eye and it would be sat in her seat at the table beside her. That's how it happened. That's how it goes for everyone. Her grandad had only died a few years ago and he was old. He was old but he would always tell stories of when he was a kid like it was yesterday. Like everything after that was just part of the deal.

Gnomes

She lived in a bungalow up Westgate. One of the ones right at the bottom that look like they're flat pack, made from big concrete slabs that slot together. I remember she used to ride around everywhere on one of them old chopper bikes with a back on the seat and the right big handlebars. And she'd always wear these men's boxer shorts that were dead baggy and, like, one of them vest tops. I mean, all the time. Winter, summer, spring. And her garden, you shoulda seen it. The most gnomes you've ever seen in your life. You don't see these gnome freaks much anymore but, at one point, every village and town had at least one person who had hundreds of the little fuckers on their garden. Course, the kids used to come and mess with them. Yer know, move them around and put them in rude positions. And, of course, she always knew EXACTLY where they shoulda been. I can see her now, running around, sorting them out with her chopper rested against the wall, poking the arse of her men's boxers up in the air when she bent over. And, her hair. Such a wild white mop.

Anyway, I never told anyone this but, I saw her one day. She was riding round the back of the old Safeway and I was going the same way to my car. She had a gnome under her arm at the time, an old beat up one that'd faded and whose fishing rod had snapped. He wasn't a glamorous old fella but I could see why she liked him, yer know, he had character. Then, I watched her as she rode to the far corner of the car park. The corner where the taxis take you at night if it don't look like you're gonna pay up. And she lent her bike on the fence, stood up on it and clambered over. I had to see what was over there, you know how nosey I am. I got in my car and drove over, pulled up and got out. I went over to the fence and clawed my weight up until I could just peep over. It was a gnome Nirvana. A pint sized Shangri-La. A porcelain Eden. But she clocked me straight away so I dropped down. She popped up on the other side and called me. *You're Karen's lad, aren't ya? Yeah. What you doin stickin yer nose in ovver here for? Ah were just avin a look. Ah not dob ya in or owt. Too right, ya not. It's none of your business. Yer shunt of even looked ovver here. Well, if it means owt, I really do think it's nice. Oh, pull the other one, yer cheeky fucker. No, really. It's . . . beautiful. I don't know much about art but I reckon that's what it is. Can I have another look?* She wasn't impressed but took a while to come back with an answer. *Well . . . I suppose you've seen it now. Hop ovver.*

I stepped up onto the chopper that swayed under my weight and clumsily chucked a leg over. I hung down, making sure that there were no little fellas under my feet before I let go. Looking around me, I saw it was all boarded up with fences and no actual way to get in. I'd say 10ft by 10ft if I had to but I'm not too good with measurements. The car park was obviously on one side, houses on two of the others and the fourth was a factory and each fence was made of a slightly different coloured panel. She'd built a pond, she'd potted up a mixture of flowers that were fully in bloom and she'd somehow managed to build a surreal miniature village with everything out of proportion with everything else. She'd even added a spire to a dog kennel for a church. *I buy that many new gnomes that I need a retirement village for the old codgers. I cun't throw em away. How'd you find this spot?* She shrugged. *Can't remember. It's mad how this little bit of land in the middle of town's been left.* She seemed to ignore me and wasn't impressed with me getting all enthusiastic on her. *And what you've done is amazing.* There was nothing from her. *I mean, truly beautiful.* She pulled a sandwich bag of worms from inside the kennel and lifted the top of a bird box next to her. Pulling long worms out and dropping them into what I can only imagine was a chick's nest.

For the next ten minutes I tried to get her attention but she ignored everything that I said. Standing so tall around all the little gnomes, I felt huge. Vulgar. A monster. And this was what she wanted. I was sure of it. I jumped back over and got into my car. Everything was noisy. The car. The people. Even the size of everything seemed noisy somehow. I opened the door at home and saw the staircase in front of me. It made me sick. There was no need for my house to ascend to the sky. Even my clothes. When I caught sight of myself in the mirror, they seemed suffocating. Dull. Tight. I stripped down to my underwear to feel the air and stepped into the front garden. The front was better than the back. Small. Manageable. With a breeze. I'd never have managed with the back.

I sat there in a deck chair until nightfall and eventually couldn't hold the urge any longer. I walked this time. In my slippers and pants. With my Skeg deck chair under my arm.

When I got to the car park, I hopped over and pulled open my deck chair next to the pond. I sat like a madman with a bottle of water and a carrot and smiled. All the gnomes around me were understanding. Reassuring. They'd seen the world like I had and ended up here too. The next thing I knew, I woke up with coppers climbing over the fence. She'd called them and told them I'd been pinching her gnomes. Can you believe it? Everything was cleared up that day so that I had to learn to live in the big world again. I still get a bit overwhelmed, at least a couple of times a day. And she smiles as she rides past me now but never says anything. I'm sure she's got another spot sorted out but I haven't found it yet. I bet it's somewhere in the woods though. Yeah, that spot round the back of the graveyard, I haven't tried there yet; it'd be perfect.

The Picture

Should we take this picture as still? The fallen tree in the foreground, the whole woodland. That would be still. But the boys with bikes to their side in the bracken, cheering; they're not still. I can hear them. And the one in the air, on his bike, the one soaring from a makeshift wooden ramp, no helmet, his hair pushed back with the wind. Is he still? His heart is beating even as we gaze at it. The trees are so high above them and they're small and at the bottom of the photo. They were never the kind of kids to sit at home and do what they were told regardless of what they will turn into. Whatever they have turned into. Everything is in front of them and they're cheering for their friend. He could be the best on a bike or the worst of them and it wouldn't matter. I took this picture fifteen years ago and I can't remember taking it. I've got more and I can't remember taking any of them. I've got so many pictures and they're all of childhood. Nothing interests me about adult life. Pictures of adults remain still, they don't breathe and move like these do. But that's the thing, they don't just breathe. If you believe in the pictures then they can do more than that. I've spent months inside of photos before, I've entered them and become part of them. The test is like this. If you put the picture flat on the floor with no glass and no frame, then dip a naked toe onto the surface, if it ripples like water then you can enter. Then you can sink your leg in and feel for something solid to take your weight. You can follow with the other leg. You can dip your head right down and enter the scene and see it move as soon as you land. With this picture, as soon as my ears pass the level I hear cheering followed by a skid and a tumble. Never once did I imagine that he wouldn't land the jump. There's a brown Labrador dropping a stick at my feet and I hear *MATE, CAN YOU HELP MATE?* So I

throw the stick for the dog and walk over to the lads who are looking down on their friend. Two of them are serious and the other
one is laughing. I'm going to be in this one for a while, I can tell.

The Thinker

This man I once knew was the one that made me lose the plot a bit. Well not really him but, well, it wouldn't have happened if I hadn't met him. He was THE stand-up guy in the village; he didn't walk around with a can of beer in his hand and no-one ever once heard him shouting. A real kind sort that you don't see very often. Everyone got on with him, they'd shout and swear at each other but when this man, Peter, walked past they'd stop and say: *Alright Peter, good to see you mate, take it easy, yeah.* And he'd smile and say thank you and walk on. I'm making him sound like a do gooder but he wasn't. He went to parties and did what other people did. I thought he was a bit simple when I first met him but when you really get talking to him it turns out he's a thinker; one of those real thinkers who can really work stuff out. I'd been talking to him whenever we were out with the same crowd and eventually I got to going round his house a bit. He lived on the side of the road that's got the field leading on from the back garden. We'd have a cup of tea and really talk. It might not seem odd to other people but round here it's hard to find someone to have a proper conversation with, like about the world and stuff. I was new to thinking and he was seasoned so he questioned me all the time, telling me that this is how I'll find out what I really believe and saying about Socrates and stuff.

In the middle of the field that his house backed onto he showed me something one day, a small opening that you could just squeeze through, in the middle of the barley, that led down to this cave of hard stone with a texture of sandpaper. It was all wet and smelt a bit like a pub. We went right down and the smell got worse. Almost mushroomy. And that was when we saw it. A little old hunched up man in a cage. You'll understand why I lost the plot. I mean, I knew there and then that I'd not be the same person again when I came back out. Peter lit a fag and just watched me with a smile. He looked more confident than I'd ever seen him look before. I was straight and asked him, *The fuck's goin off here, mate?* The hunched man seemed to flinch at my voice. He was nearly naked. Peter told me the hunched old man was the last of the *closed-caskets*. I didn't know what he meant when he said that so I asked him and he said he'd been studying them and they lived in the woods and they'd spend a lot of time under-ground like slugs or moles, digging around and living off of grubs and stuff but also feeding on dead animals and bones and even the dead bodies in the graveyard and that's why they were called closed-caskets. Cos they've got teeth that can bite through nails. People used to hunt them at night and they thought they were all gone, it's lucky that witches like Karen from the Quad were still putting spells on people's houses to protect them, that's what he told me, but that wouldn't last for ever. I ignored the fact that Karen was a witch and I told him he'd lost the plot and, to clear things up, I asked if he was saying this man was like a fairy or a woodland creature or something and he said something like that but he didn't know much more about him at the minute. I was having a hard time believing all of this and I had to raise my voice with him, it was hard but I said, *Peter, what the fuck are you doing, pal?* He told me that he found him in here and he didn't put him in the cage and he didn't know what to do, that's why he brought me down. He said that he thought we were mates and asked me why I was being so aggressive. I felt bad about raising my voice and told him so. I don't think Pete had ever been spoken to like that; no-one wants to be mad at Peter.

I sat down on a rock and said, *OK, OK, let's come up with a plan. I stood up and started pacing.*

We can either   ermmm well   leave it here and
pretend we never found it   or   or like,   ring the police or
*   summet   or   fuckin kill it.   Like whack it on the head with*
a rock or summet.

Pete was too nice for all of this and shook his head. I'd snapped. I could tell he'd brought me down here to make all of the decisions. Pete was a thinker, not a doer. That's why he'd never had a job. I asked, *Well does Golem fuckin talk?* He didn't answer me so I asked the creature, *Do you fuckin talk, Golem? Look, here's my ring, you want it?* Peter told me not to wind him up, he was sheepish and very uncomfortable. He told me that I'd make it angry but it was too late, I already had. It went mad in the cage, it rattled and jumped and with one bite it took a chunk from a metal bar. I just ran. I grabbed Pete as I went past and we ran straight back to his house and locked and bolted the door and stared out of the kitchen window that overlooked the field. Quietly. Pete ran the tap and I asked what he was doing and he told me he was putting the kettle on. I nodded, *good idea.*

The brew did help to calm the nerves and we started talking like normal again. Well I did. Pete was still a bit quieter than before. I asked him how long he'd known about it and he said he'd been feeding it for a couple of years now. He got his phone out and showed me pictures of these snares and traps he'd built for catching animals. He said that sometimes he'd sit and eat with it. It'd rip apart a squirrel raw and Pete would sit there with like a chicken kiev or panini and eat with him. He showed me a painting, 'Saturn Devouring His Son', and that was exactly what it looked like. He said it helped him to sit with the closed-casket and see himself as 'animal'.

★

Pete was found dead a few months later. The police looked into it and it turned out he'd been skipping treatment for a cancerous tumour. Everyone was talking about it. His death affected the community and, as no-one knew his family, I was getting a lot of the commiserations which felt weird. I know it's mad but I'd carried on Pete's snaring and was chucking food down this hole. One day I even made a panini but couldn't bring myself to go in and see if the creature had come back. There could have been a huge pile of rotting animals down there for all I knew. I thought of how Pete could be hiding in the cave and eating it all and laughing at everyone thinking he was dead just because they'd seen his body. He got you questioning things, Pete did, even after he was gone. He always asked what I'd do if I knew I didn't have long left to live and I'd assumed he was trying to get me to think without 'boundaries' or something but it was really because he knew he was going to die. I don't think I ever gave him any real help on that one. He was the thinker, not me.

That's where the story ended until a sign went up outside of Pete's old house one day. AUCTION. There were to be no viewings, the house came as it was left due to Pete having no family to clear it all out. The only pictures on the website were of the kitchen. I was curious and all of the commiserations must have gone to my head because I felt a right to see what was in there and take anything valuable. The things that were valuable to Pete would probably end up in a skip if the next person was left to decide.

It was easy to get in. I had a hammer in my pocket but the old wooden back door went through with a quick kick. Being stood there was a strange feeling, the last time I'd been in that kitchen we'd fled for our lives and now it seemed quieter than anything.

In the living room, the floorboards were black and covered with rat droppings that had been trodden down over time. There was nothing else in the room apart from a single seater settee that had been chewed up and a tall lamp behind that was still left switched on. I could hear the rats underneath the floorboards scratching and scuttling and I could feel the floor moving. A couple of them popped up and ran towards me. I slammed the door on them, then breathed in deep before turning to the stairs and working my way up. It looked like upstairs was his space for studying. There were loose pages and books that lined the floors. There were symbols that even the rats were afraid of. And the walls. They were paintings. The sun and the moon were painted on either end of the landing. On the sun side there was the bathroom and an empty box room; the walls tattooed with stories that were almost hieroglyphs. I studied them, touched them, put my cheek to them. On the moon side was his bedroom. A dark room with flattened cardboard boxes on the floor for a bed, a loose sheet and a pillow. The walls were painted black. It was clearly a tunnel, textured like jagged soil and stone. As you looked left from the door, the tunnel started and continued around the windowless room until, there it was. A study in all its detail. The creature. Its features so crisp that my breath was sucked from me, I could see it breathing and smell its stench. It was impossible to tell if it was a painting or if it was alive. Either way, it was captured on the wall. The hammer was heavy in my pocket. I took it out and began. It was a mess. I washed my hands, peeled the hieroglyph wallpaper from the walls carefully, rolled it up and left. I could hang it up at home and begin my study. I had a lot of work to do.

The Fog

The fog was thick all that week. So thick that when you looked out of your front window, you couldn't see the road past your garden. People spoke about the fog in the same way that a heavy downpour is or a really hot spell in summer, but this was different. You couldn't tell whether you were coming or going. And people kept getting lost, mainly older people and when they finally got back they'd be ragged and saying how the fog had tunnels that went on forever and they'd get manic when their son or daughter would say *Alright Mavis, let's get you a cup of tea and some toast and everything will be alright.* But it wasn't only them, the hippy lot all said that it was a sign of something, the Christians were split, some went on about chemical warfare but most people just thought it was thick fog. I must admit, at the time, I thought it was thick fog.

My own story starts when I was walking the dog one morning that week. I was only taking the little madam around the block for a quick pittle, there was no way I was going anywhere I'd not usually go. Oh, she was tugging on the lead and pulling me round like she usually does, the stocky little bogger, and it was so thick that I could only see the garden wall at my left hand and the end of the curb on my right. There were the screams of crows and jackdaws in the air, I mean those really creepy CAWWW sounds. I was telling myself to stop being daft for panicking and I ran my hand along the crumbled brick top and watched the fog glide through my fingertips and felt it brush my skin and when I looked to my right, the curb had vanished. I walked towards it. One pace, two, three, four, well past where the end drop should be, taking those steps that are prepared for a fall. I bent down to see the ground and found hard dirt around my feet; compacted and brown, not the asphalt that should be coarse on my fingers. I looked back and could no longer see the wall. There was only white fog dancing like static. I took another, six, seven, eight paces, looked around and saw a chain on the floor. I must have put the dog's lead down when I touched the dirt, I can't remember doing it but it was definitely there. It pulled away suddenly and was gone. I shouted for her as loud as I could but knew she wouldn't come back. Doing what she's told isn't her style. I hugged my coat tighter around me and looked in every direction for a sign but all I could see was blindness. I used my head as a magnet and let it turn to the place it wanted to stop and walked, hoping I would bump into something, someone or anything to give me a sense of some kind. At this point, I think it's needless to say, there was a great deal of worry. My heart had sunk and I felt like I could vomit, I must make this clear, but I get so focused on not panicking in tight situations that I find these parts hard to recall sometimes and delve straight into the action. I looked to see if there were any signs of the sun trying to burn through. I hadn't left my own street I was sure of that. It took me a while to tune into but it sounded like a woman's voice. I shouted back as loudly as I could and she said to follow the sound of her horn and she pressed the horn like beep beep beep beeeeeeeeeeeep, then repeating it. It was difficult to latch onto. Every time I went to shout, another BEEP cut me off. It was frustrating but my only hope was to keep on trying. It felt like hours with not one more word from the person just this beep beep beeeeeeeeep and I got so fed up that I sat on the ground and as soon as I did the horn stopped. I was glad in a way until I heard: *You made it!* and saw three shadows in front of me through the white. Silhouettes that looked like a puppet show. It was a crisp blur of car, person, tree. There was a smirk and a lack of panic even though he was supposed to be lost. He said *Thank god, I dunno how I got here, I was driving round for what felt like days and now my car's out of diesel and I don't know what to do.* I asked why he was smiling and never thought that he should be a woman from how his voice sounded before and he told me that he was just happy to see another person. His car was quite nice, a really big family car. In the window of it, I saw my reflection. A mottled, wilted, poor version of myself and I heard myself ask if he'd seen a dog. He hadn't but he had heard barking, wasn't sure how long ago and asked me what the dog's name was and what breed it is and made me look like a liar because I couldn't remember either and when I told him that he laughed and said *typical*. I gazed deeper into the glass of the car until I noticed the tree behind me and all the bodies hanging from it on ropes and the bloke stood there was smiling, only now with a fag in his teeth, flicking his zippo open and rolling his finger down it with a crunch. He felt like a noir character the way he bit his fag. The flame of the lighter looked so yellow, like it was the first colour I had seen in so long. It hissed as the fog moved and got thicker suffocating the flame. I asked about the people hanging from the tree and he said *what people* and when he closed his zippo the bodies were gone. I don't know if I need to say this, but I didn't trust this man.

It wasn't until this point that I noticed that the fog had been lifting. Not lifting as in getting thinner, more the fact that there was no fog to about knee height. It seems bizarre when I look back but all I remember is that I'd had enough of this guy so I got onto all fours and then there was colour; green grass lit by sunshine somehow and in front of me, where the car and person were, there was nothing. The bottom of the tree was there with its roots and stuff, but no person. I didn't want to poke my head back up but I closed my eyes and pushed through the fog and breathed, one-two then opened them and there he was, right there, his face right up to mine and he said *Where you going after all this time sweetheart?* His teeth were black and his skin was grey. I did what seemed natural somehow, don't peg me as a wrong un but I pushed him in his chest as hard as I could and ducked back down to the peaceful place. When I did, the dog was peeing up the tree. Can you believe it? I yelled *Jess* and she came tootling over like nothing had happened, her chain jingling as it dragged on the ground, and licked my face with her tail going like the clappers. I still couldn't tell you what breed that little mongrel is to be honest.

Turns out we were about two miles away from home now that I look back and, yeah, we crawled all the way. I was fucked when I got back. John asked where I'd been and I looked at him with my mouth open. He asked again, said he'd been worried. I looked out the window, the fog had lifted half way up the glass now. It was going. There was no point being Mavis. I said, *Leave me alone John, I'm not in the mood for this right now.*

It'd be no use telling a bloke anyway.

The Word

There's a word I once heard that had no meaning at all; a strange word that this man taught me. He said you could use it anywhere and, because it means nothing so strongly, people will hear the word, (or read the word even) the word that they want to. The word that they think is there. It took him a few months to teach me because it takes practise to even be able to start hearing it in the first place, let alone being able to use it effectively. Now I use it all the time, throw it into conversations when I'm stuck for what to say. For all you know, this could be written solely using that word. You'd never know. You could have created this whole story up yourself by a freak coincidence and someone else could pick it up and say that it was stupid cos *How did they even breathe on Mars?* or something like that. But I haven't done that so don't start reading back. You see, it's a bit like the way I imagine learning kung fu would be after watching too much telly. You're *supposed* to only use it when you need to. But because I know how to hear it, I see all of those who use it: overuse it. Or use it for gain. Think of politicians, for example. It's a perfect tool for them. You'd be glad to hear that they didn't know the word, and I'd tell you that if only it was true. But it's not. They spout it left, right and centre, if you get my drift.

I only tend to use it in really minor situations, really. For example, last week I had my mum and my mate round and I managed to ask one if we're picking up any weed and the other if I could put off fitting their cat flap until the next day. There's not really any chance of me using it for any real trouble. That's probably why he chose me, I suppose.

The Pond

It was the first time I'd ever really tried gardening. I mean, I've mown the grass since I was a kid but I've never really gardened. In fact, I'd say I've actively avoided anything that looked like gardening for most of my life but I thought I'd give it a go anyway. It was 2017 and this place was home and home should have something that resembles a garden. What I was remembering the most was the pond we had as a kid. I'd spend months of my life gazing into it and watching the tadpoles develop, trying to find that elusive newt that was there once and lifting stones to find squealing frogs. We even ended up with a fish, don't ask me how but we did. And this is why I've got the shovel in my hand. I was getting ready for the next chapter. Sprogs. Those little feet that make you laugh and cry and tear your hair out and it was bound to happen at some point and by then I wanted frogs and all we had at the minute was this rectangle of grass and six foot fences. Not inspiring for frogs or sprogs. The garden got waterlogged a lot in winter and that was because of the clay soil. I found that out on my first dig. It wasn't easy lifting it out. But I got to thinking. I had nowhere to put all of this clay and I'd seen a program on the telly about tribes making huts with it so with each dig I started building up next to the hole. It was going to be a round structure with a door- way, nothing fancy, sort of like a clay igloo. I was mixing in all bits of old copper pipes and things to make it sturdy, things left lying around from doing the house up and for whatever reason it was working. By the end of the first day I had a circle about 10 foot across and 2 foot high. My girlfriend kept coming out and telling me how it was a stupid idea but I didn't care. The next few days were the same, I just cracked on with it. The pond was now getting huge but it was a means to an end. I tried making a snake shape with the hole but all of the ends kept joining together and by the end of the first week, half the garden was dug for a pond and the hut was up to head high and feeling more rigid than I could have imagined. Sarah made it clear to me that she was ringing her family and was going to tell them that she thinks I've gone mad but I pretended I didn't hear her. She was still going out and doing the shopping and everything as normal and I was out there digging and building for as long as my back would let me. She invited some of our friends around one night and Steve thought it was amazing but Carol was like my Mrs, she thought the whole thing was a bit bizarre. I told her that I was going to plant bamboo and build a little bridge and stuff and that it'd look really nice and then she asked me what the point of the hut was and I hadn't really thought about that bit. I tried not to make it obvious to Sarah so I said that it could be a play house for a kid and that made them both coo but I knew Sarah was just playing along. I finally got the lid on my hut about a week later and there was still grass and space so while Sarah was at work, I started another hut opposite the first one and carried on digging. I knew then that there'd have to be a boat to get to the huts. A little boat that was moored near the house.

Sarah was fuming when she got home and saw the pile of slabs I'd took up, sitting in the living room watching telly. She said she didn't want a swamp for a garden and that it'd come to the point where she had to stop me. I told her to believe in me but she said if I carried on she was leaving and she did leave. I was so focussed that I didn't really notice at first but she definitely had left because I used to use her hairbrush after a shower and it wasn't there anymore. I tried to keep straight when I was working. It was getting to where this hunch was taking shape. Then we got hit with some serious rain. It'd been glorious weather for weeks so I hadn't thought about how it'd hold up. It rained all night. Nailed it down. And I was there. By the window of the back bedroom. Watching. I wish now that it'd washed all away and I could've forgot about it. But it held up pretty well.

The walls were still intact, I just had to patch up a few minor holes in the roof. I painted the dome with bitumen and that was that.

Around three weeks later, the second hut was up and both of them stood on islands, the rest of the garden was completely dug down. The pond got lined and, without a hosepipe, I could turn the outside tap on and let it fill. I'd already bought a small, blow up dingy to get from one side to the other. In the long term I'd build a wooden raft but that would do for now. Steve came round when it was filling. I got him a can and he shook his head as he saw it all. He called me mental in a half joking way and said I could've at least put some stepping stones in or something. I admitted, that would've been a good idea but I was happy with what I'd achieved. I told him how I'd get some trout to put in and then I can fish out of the hut and eat it on a fire out there if I didn't fancy coming in for some food. He said he couldn't believe what he was hearing, that he couldn't believe I was going to use it. I said I was going to live out there. Wash my clothes in the water, sleep there, have dreams there, then I told him there was another hut if he wanted to join me. Of course he said no, he had a wife and everything but I knew he'd come around. He started visiting more and more when everything was in place. It turned into a bit of a mangrove with the trees. It was great. Until the council came for their routine inspection, didn't they. They weren't just angry about the garden. They were angry that I'd spent all my time on this instead of looking for a job. I told them that I only wanted it to feel like home and they asked if I was a drug user. There was no reasoning with them. They asked me to come out from my hut, into the kitchen. I refused. I could see Steve in the back of his hut in his pants with clay smeared on his face but they couldn't from their angle. He looked scared. I refused to come out and was clear that I felt no wrong had been done and that I was entitled to make my home feel more like a home. Plus, I said, I've only added value to the property, surely. They said that my eviction notice would be in the post and said that they take it my partner had long left and I ignored them.

Steve came out after they'd gone. He asked how long he'd been here. I wasn't sure, couldn't tell. By the look of him and the tribal smears on his face and torso, it was weeks. Time can sometimes be strange like that. And now, me and Steve were the first tribe in this town for thousands of years. I said that I wasn't sure but that I thought I had an idea and Steve was ready, he was a panicker that needed me to be the voice of reason. I started talking and he leant forward. I told him that we need to take our clothes off and that we need to get into the water. We need to swim and we need to get our bodies more adapted to the water and if we learn to hold our breath for longer periods of time then we could hide from any threats. He nodded in agreement that it was probably the best course of action so we stripped down and got into the water. We learnt to hold our breath for longer and longer which only blurred time more. We went from spending hours under there to days and, maybe longer. There was no real need to come back out, we had everything we needed. And our bodies started adapting too, our feet were becoming webbed and our mouths broader, our skin turned slimey and green.

One day, kids came onto the garden and got into the boat. They paddled across and took sides on either hut. I told Steve that it wasn't right to have kids here while we were still working things out. We needed to go up and tell them to get lost, they can't come in and destroy our home so we both jumped up out of the water. The kids looked round and went, Whoa! and picked us up and held us really close to their faces. We tried to jump away but they wouldn't let us. They held on tight and really gave us the once over then put us back down in the pond. I told Steve that I thought I'd gone too far and he said ribbit and left and he had a point, life was actually quite good down here.

One Toke

One toke. I'll just have one. I stopped smoking it when I was younger cos I used ta get all parra, like I had cockroaches crawling under my skin nd that, you know what I mean? No. Probably just me being a fucking weirdo then. It were always good fun nd that but then one day it just stopped being. I was baked with all the lads and I saw this little axe on the side and couldn't stop worrying about someone just picking it up and sinking it into me skull, mate. Fucked up shit like that. If I just have one toke, I just get dead chatty and people can't get a word in, not that they can anyway. It's like, I was thinking the other night, about that time when we were pissing off that big aqueduct or whatever it was when we were fucked and Peaty fucking slipped nd we had to all pull him up, mate, he coulda died then. And then that time we were throwing them bricks up onto the bridge from the train station just to see if we could make it up there and then one did nd we just heard a car screech and ran to fuck. Never even thought that there were cars nd people up there. Mate, when we were off our heads like that we were dangerous, the amount of times people coulda died. But no-one did, I suppose that's a bonus. Fuck me, pal, I'm fucked up. One toke! One fucking toke. That shit must be radioactive. Either that or I'm just a fucking lightweight. That's a more likely story. I don't smoke anymore mate. I just go down town nd see what's about. Can't keep a good looking lad like me away from the ladies, wun't be right. Gotta give the world it's bitta loving, ant I? Hah! Fuckin hell, that were strong.

Paul

I don't know who the woman was that I always used to use as the women in my daydreams, she was probably from, like, my mind's stock images. She looked friendly, comfortable with me, like we'd been together a long time and that her little heart made my face melt. But also like a real woman. Something way off what I could ever hope for. A bit like a woman in an old film who wears a classy dress and a longing gaze. But, these are the kind of places your mind takes you on the 92 bus to work. The one that goes the long way around all of the houses. That's the only bus that goes past mine. It's alright over summer though, without the kids coming back from school. I don't have to hear about 'Johnny whacking Pete' or 'Leanne getting off with Big Steve the mechanic' or whatever it happens to be.

My mum stopped making me sandwiches for work a couple of weeks ago. She never said she was going to stop, she just did and I didn't say anything either. I checked the fridge a couple of times and saw her look at me. My dad never said anything either but he's all but stopped talking altogether now, anyway. It's like he's saving his voice for this big occasion that he knows about but won't tell us. That would make sense, I suppose, if he didn't look so defeated. I try to be friendly and pat him on the back like 'son of the year' or a son that watches the footy and he does do a half smile that looks like it could shatter him in two. I haven't got a clue what's got him like this. I tried to talk about it once but my mum said *PAUL* in this really stern voice and my dad didn't say anything so I went to my room.

My line of work is like my mum's. Well, she doesn't work anymore but she cleans a lot, like, compulsively. And that's what I do. I clean offices and stuff after they're closed up for the day. I hoover, dust, mop the toilet. I've got my routine mapped out to a T and I don't have to go back on myself once throughout the whole shift because of it. The other cleaners were angry at first, I could tell; thought that I was going to make them look bad but no-one cares either way so they let me do most of the work now. I don't mind, it keeps me busy and I kind of enjoy it. I make up games like I would when I was younger, pretending the duster is a car skidding over the desks and stuff.

I like it best when you go onto a floor that's been empty for a while and the lights are all out. They're all sensored now so I can walk through and watch my reflection in the window as they ding ding ding on above me. The lights are white yellow in here but when you look to the street they're duller and keep a lot more shadows. I've caught loads of animals out of the windows: foxes, bats, owls, badgers.

I go down to the courtyard on my break to eat my sandwiches but today I've got a salad box from the corner shop. I was trying to be healthy but I can't really eat much because the lettuce has gone all soggy and the mayo has sort of separated. All the other staff are women and they tend to stand away from me, smoking and chatting. Hazel, the younger one, often shouts stuff over to make the others laugh. About me being Mr Muscle or Speedy Gonzalez, usually. I sorta snort to not look mardy but I always go red. It helps that these lights are duller so they don't notice.

I like Hazel. She holds a look at me without saying anything. I've never really had anyone do that before. I'd like to take her out for lunch or something but I can't ask out of the blue so I'm waiting for the right chance. We were alone once and I should have asked her then. We got locked in a small office by the older lot for a laugh who shouted something about wanting babies to be there when we got out. She was telling me how, when she was a kid, she would lock herself into a room with her favourite teddy and they'd have to work out how they could escape. She said it was the teddy that always had all of the good ideas. I can't remember what I said back. I just remember her pulling my apron over my head and giggling. I've never been with a woman before. The thought of it seems impossible. That's probably why I'm so into dinosaurs still.

On the way home, I'm sat on the night bus which hasn't left the station yet. I forget it's a Friday till I see two bald men waddle with arms over each others' shoulders, swaying as they get on the bus. I look out of the window and there's a woman squatting and peeing up a lamp post while her mates try to huddle around and hide her. The bus is starting to pull off and I see Hazel running up the slope and waving. I stand up to go and tell the bus driver that there's someone coming and he must stop but as I stand the driver stops anyway and open the doors, saying *C'mon love, can't have you stuck on yer own at this time, can we?* Next thing I hear, *You must've sprinted up here, Speedy Gonzalez.* I laugh a bit and feel my cheeks burning when she sits next to me. She starts rolling a fag and catches me looking at her. *Want one? Yeah, please.* I think I'll be alright because I used to go round Gary's and smoke weed and play on his X-Box so I know how to smoke. *I thought your boyfriend gave you a lift? Yeah, he did, but he's not my boyfriend now so I think a lift's out of the question.* I stay quiet, not to pry but she carries on anyway. *That slag Emma Barlow, that's who it was. Him fingering her in The Half Moon smoking shelter ten minutes before I got there. I felt like SUCH a twat.* She hands me the fag and starts to roll the next one. I can hardly ask her out now, can I? She looks up with a frown, *I know you can be fun Paul, I've seen you acting daft and that, loosen up. What about we go for a drink?* I fumble for words: *Err, yeah, alright.*

She doesn't take me to The Half Moon, that'd be weird. Instead we get off the bus and head to The Seven Stars. I wonder if she knows that my house is only round the corner or if it's a coincidence. She seems to know the barman and he pours us both a pint. I stare at his ponytail in the mirror behind him, he looks too big and muscley to have a ponytail somehow. He looks to me and asks *What's your story then fella?* And I don't know what to say so I just shrug, *Not a lot interesting about me.* Hazel smiles with her pint to her lips, *I bet there is, Paul, c'mon then, what's the maddest thing you've done?* The barman shouts to everyone about last orders being over and everyone nods. I watch him lock the door and start dishing out ashtrays. When I turn back around, Hazel's lighting her roll up and still staring at me: *Well. Go on then.* I grab the lighter and take a drag on mine, splutter a bit and say, *I once took magic mushrooms and went fishing.* She sort of half spits her drink out when I say this, *You, what? Who with?* She asks. *On my own*, I say. *On yer chuffing own!* She looks around like it's the maddest thing she's heard, like she can't believe what she's hearing and it sort of relaxes me. *See, I knew you were a mad head really, I can tell. Did you catch the Loch Ness Monster or something?* She laughs at herself. Hazel's one of these people who's the same with everyone. *I never actually made it to the pond, to be honest. It was dark and I felt like the trees were out to get me. I ran all the way back home, it felt like I was on a treadmill and the world moved towards me.* She asked me, *Where did you get em?* I tell her that *I picked them on the cricket pitch. I've got a book that tells you what to look for, grey gills, a nipple on top.* She stops me, *Nipples, now we're talking.*

When we get outside after the drink, I ask her, *Hazel, do you ever feel like you're not cut out for it all?* She smiles at me and puts her arm over my shoulder, leading me down the road. *I think you'll find that there's not many people who are actually cut out for it all, Pauly.* I say, *I think you're right. My parents definitely aren't.* She leads me down a multitude of streets and I never once ask where we're going, it's just comfortable somehow. Then she stops and opens a gate between two buildings. In the gennel she unlocks the front door on the left. Her flat's on the ground floor and I'm impressed that she even has her own place. It's a bedroom, kitchen, dining room all in one combo with the only other room being the bathroom. It feels nice in here. It's clean but full of little bits that catch your eye, all over the walls and shelves and stuff. She watches me looking around for a bit and says, *I go to a lot of carboots and buy tat.* But it's not tat, everything looks like her somehow. She grabs a bottle of rum and two glasses and sits on the bed, leaning on the headboard. I sit at the bottom and she pours one and hands it to me.

I like you, Paul, she says, *you're a real thinker.* She says it with pride that she's worked me out and I quite like it. Thinker. Yeah, that's me. And I say, *I've always liked you, Hazel, you make everyone smile.* And I can tell that she likes that one. She moves forward and grabs my face. Her lips are soft and she smells like fresh laundry and cigarettes. *I'm not going to have sex with you, Paul, but we can spoon if you want to keep me warm tonight?* And she smiles. I know that means she'll never have sex with me but I like the idea of spooning.

Witch Play

I say that I've come to see Jack at the little table that the great fat lady is sat behind with her inflatable arms bouncing at her sides and see her eyes look around to ask if mum or dad has come as well, in that annoying little patter that ses she's worked with young kids for faaaaar too long and would rather be with them than adults. She knows the fucking answer as I say how they couldn't make it, unfortunately, and pop her over an intentionally over eager smile. She just wanted to hear me say it I reckon. She knows that them two were never gonna come. The first time she dealt with me I think she was worried that I was the mother, I could see it in her face. What, I'd have to gave birth when I was like four, duck. Fuck this biddy anyway. Walk to the hall and take a programme off of the seat and sit. Flick through the pages to see if there's a pic of our Jack: there's not. There's a full cast list at the back and right near the bottom there's: CARETAKER – JACK SEWELL. It makes me heart jump to see it and I think of seeing him all dressed up last night with penned stubble on his face. He was in character all night, being a right little bloke, not that he'd know what a bloke did. He pretended to go to the shop for a paper, sat with one leg over the other pretending to read it, then got and cracked a pretend can of beer outta the fridge, big AHHHH and wiped his mouth with the back of his hand. I kept asking him where he got these ideas of what a man does but he was so in character that he wouldn't accept that he wasn't a man. I'll make sure he becomes a good one though. Me n Jack. That's all there is at the minute. I even turned me phone off last night, we were having that much fun dicking about. Wrighty kept blabbing on about me coming out and stuff but I couldn't be arsed with it. Turned me fuckin phone on this morning and had loadsa messages about how

I was a slag anyway and how he was going to get with Chantelle because she's got better tits.

The lights go down and I hold me breath. Not too much, like, cos I had a look at the script and he don't come in till about three quarters of the way through so I know I've got a bit of a wait and like, I don't think I'm going to, but I start getting right into it. The main character's played by this right mouthy girl who thinks she can sing and that and she's not too bad but I can tell that I'd not get on with her but once you get past that and just take her for what she is, it's alright. She's meant to be a woman from the past who goes travelling around villages but they all think that she's a witch so she has to run off before they burn her at the stake but then she gets to one place and decides that they need her help so she starts giving out potions and stuff and bit by bit everyone's problems are getting solved but what they don't know is that they aren't really potions and that when they think that they can get on and be nice to everyone they DO. The town start being nice to the tramp and he ends up being, like, really good at fixing things and becomes a big part of the village and everyone likes him then and when everyone is nice to everyone else it all goes smoothly until she starts telling people that she can't give them a potion and telling them what's really going off. The people don't believe her and they all decide that they're going to burn her for being a witch cos she WON'T give em the potions! The fuck's up with that? The only person that understood from the start was the local school teacher and I almost forget that Jack's in it when she goes looking around the school for him, like, I almost forget that I'm watching a play at all, and Jack's there sweeping up when she goes in and asks him *Where's Paul? I really need to see him* and Jack ses *Don't ask me, I'm just the janitor* and I wonder if the other parents notice the waver in his voice or the way his hand shakes as he runs it across his forehead in the background. And, a tear comes to my eye as I'm so proud of Jack for doing such a good job as he fumbles down the steps but my heart is still racing cos she's gotta find Paul, he's her only hope to not get burned and to save the town from themselves, why can't they see what they're doing, why are people so blind? And when she does find Paul he tells her how the people are always going to be like this, that it's inevitable, but I don't think he really thinks this deep down, it's just what he's always known but he agrees to help her anyway cos any idiot in the audience can see that he loves her and you can hear the mob shouting and approaching the school while they're still talking and I see the kids lining up off stage to come and storm the place so I know it's gonna happen soon and what are they going to do and Paul hides her in a cupboard and they come in demanding her and he points to the window and ses she's already gone and she'll be at the next village before dawn but then I hear her cough (don't cough you stupid cow!) so they know exactly where she is and when they pull it open they drag her out and all the way down to the village green to burn her. They tie her up and she's not saying anything and at this point. I think, my god, the whole thing's over now, she's done for and I was ready to let her go until she made this speech. This speech. This speech that included all of the town's names and the good things they'd done when all they'd drank was dirty puddle water and how that if they can find it in their heart to release her that it will be the first step that they can take to being the people that they all obviously want to be and all that they have to do is to believe, it doesn't take magic to find love in your heart it just takes belief and. And. They let her out. Then the crowd applaud a lame titter tatter of clappter but I'm on my feet slamming my hands together while some people look around and mutter but there's no way this was just an average play, like, not that I've seen plays, but it was more than that. I see the head teacher to one side who catches me and smiles a half-laugh like the rest of them, but fuck em, fuck em all, the kids need to know how good that was.

After the play, Jack comes over to me, still all red in the face with his thumbs tucked into his backpack. Looking up at me I tell him how good it was, how magical the play was and how he made me feel so proud and how he was the best caretaker I'd ever seen in my life. He said that there was no need to stand up and look silly but I tell him not to worry about that and I can see that he's dead proud even if he's embarrassed of me. A hand grabs me on the arm and I see the head and he tells me to come and see him tomorrow morning so I tell him I have to see the fucker every morning cos I'm on report and ask what he's on about but he leaves it at that and walks off while I look back down at Jack and slowly speak the syllables *A MAY ZING*.

Fag Ash

There was a big crash and sounds of a magnitude that were too hard to hear all in one go, that's the main thing I remember from the day that the factory exploded and the place was burnt to the ground. A single factory surrounded by houses, a warehouse in an estate of weary people and it blew up. Seems fitting somehow. They made chemicals to laminate magazines or something and everyone said it was for the insurance. They seemed to say it before it happened, they said it that quick. And as if by magic, no-one was hurt, that's what I'd be saying if all the rumours were true but they're not true and I know it. The factory was torn down the following week and in its place was left a patch of concrete with a twelve foot spiked fence around the perimeter. It's still like that now. Only, an ash tree has grown up from one of the cracks in the floor.

I feel this weird sensation that comes with a sound but tell myself it can't be real. It's every time I walk up past here. There's a faint sound coming from the house on the corner. Terry's house. No-one's seen him for years but we're still sure it's Terry's house because you'd know if it wasn't. If you listen carefully you can hear Terry tinkling the keys of a piano. He's always practising the same song. It's a song that sounds like the soundtrack to the surviving men of a medieval war walking back from battle with images of the dead imprinted on the back of their skulls and they've got blood slashed across their face and clothes. I feel like Terry must have been the soul of this place and that he has to play a song or the place will die but this is the only song that he can remember. There's space for a violin to join, I can hear the tune but I can't muster the energy to learn to play.

It's funny really. The people round here have such a sense of humour and you've chosen me to tell you about the factory and go off on a tangent about the music from Terry's house. I will tell you the story though; it's a funny story really. My uncle Pete worked there at the time so I'd sometimes be sent up when I was younger, by my grandma. Say if he'd forgot his sandwiches or something. I didn't mind because they let me drive the forklift sometimes. They'd laugh at me going round in circles and smoke just outside of the door. I was there when it happened. I was on the forklift in fact. And they were smoking in fact. And that's what the problem was. That's what the problem was when someone's dog escaped from their garden (I'm not going to speculate whose dog it was but I have heard stories) and ran up to my uncle. It was a big dog, a Great Dane or something and my uncle didn't see it coming. The dog jumped up him from behind and pushed him over and Pete's fag was flung straight out of his hand and into one of the vats. It wasn't an insurance claim but people still think it was and it killed Uncle Pete and the dog and two other people that Pete was stood with. Me and another bloke came off alright. Considering.

I wonder if other people hear that piano when they walk past Terry's house. I wonder if they all hear a different part that they could join with. I wonder if we all have our own instrument in our heads and our own part in his melody. I wonder what it would sound like if we all played together. Apparently, down the pit everyone would play instruments. I heard they'd all bring them with them, drums, flutes, tin whistles, bassoons, accordions and bagpipes. All the instruments you could imagine and that would help loosen the coal for digging. There was a reason to play music then I suppose, there's no need for me to pick up a violin nowadays. I wonder if they'll ever do anything with the strip of concrete again or just leave it with the ash tree growing.

God

I could tell straight away that he was an evergreen. It was miserable out and we were both at the bus stop in the rain and he was wearing shorts. I didn't want to know this man that waved his hands as he spoke and paced up and down the shelter and laughed with his head back. I showed enough enthusiasm to appear polite. Passable. I thought it was obvious but obviously it wasn't.

He sat next to me on the bus.

He didn't   sit across the way.

Hesatsoclosewewere touching.

Every time he moved, his raincoat crackled and made that sound that waterproofs do. A rustle maybe. His grey goatie was damp and as I looked down to his running shorts and trainers without socks, I blonked my head on the window and studied the raindrops like we've all done when we're feeling that way.

The things he talked about were of no interest to me. At all. He was into 'the world's fucked' and I've always been 'I'll leave the world alone, if the world leaves me alone'. I was a passive citizen and I liked it. But this evergreen who rabbited on like it wasn't even winter, he'd took an interest in me. He opened a can of super strength lager that I wasn't familiar with and put his other hand out towards me to introduce himself. Steve Farmer. But known as Clutch. I never asked him why he was called Clutch so I called him Steve and he told me to call him Clutch so I did after that. I was hoping he wouldn't ask me where I was going right up until the point he asked me and I panicked. I panicked and without thinking pressed the button, stood up so he got the picture and said that this is my stop and that I'm sorry but it was nice talking to him and   then   he said   me too.

Me too.

My stomach was uncomfortable and we both moved forward on the bus, the driver pulled up and we got off. I looked around and knew where I was. There were fields and dry-stone walls and an old dilapidated hut and lots of sheep. I wondered why he could possibly be out here until he lit a fag and asked me where we were going. That annoyed me but anger's not my game so I asked, *WE?* The rain had stopped for now but his hair was still damp. He shrugged and said, well, yeah. I told him that I wanted to be on my own because I did and he told me that he knew a cool place and that he'd show me to it and I was firm. I'd had enough. I told him to stop it and to go away, I told him I'd had a lot of difficult things come up at the minute and that I wasn't really looking to go hiking with someone. And he said, I know Gary. I asked how he knew my name but he just said, come, I'll show you. So I did. I followed him.

Up a ragged path.

Over a hill of divets and mounds.

(He offered me a can and I took it. It was warm and tasted thick and rancid.)

Then there was an edge, a rocky cliff face and we sat down as the low sun lit the sky orange-red. He told me he knew life had been hard lately. And I asked if he was Uncle Tony who I'd never met before and he shook his head and laughed that he'd told me his name and I said oh yeah. He was the one that was still now and I was kicking my legs and panicking although I had nowhere that I HAD to be. I never did. He took this in, looked me straight in the eye and told me he was God. This man with a can of 10% lager in his hand who's been going on about these two Jack Russells that he would take out hunting deer, he was telling me he was God. And then he told me to jump. He said, if I'm God then I'll catch you with angels and if I'm not then you'll die and no-one will be bothered. I laughed a bit and told him I'm not doing it but then I felt his hand on my back. Placed right between my shoulder blades. A firm hand. I looked into his eyes and felt tears. I said, Clutch, God, mate, don't do this please. He said, It's ok, I'll catch you. I don't know what I did to deserve it but he pushed me.

I seemed
to fall
for a
long
time,
a longer
time
than
I
should
have,
before

he caught me and pulled me back up to the top by cherubs with wings. I couldn't believe it, I said, *My God you're real* as I watched the cherubs fly off, *Oh my God*. He simply said, The world isn't as they say it is, it isn't as they say I say it is, so keep your wits about you, lad. You just gained purpose. Now can we carry onto your mate Rob's house, I fancy smoking a bong and playing X-Box and don't try and pretend that's not where you were going in the first place.

You are now leaving

The Bygones

Jim Gibson grew up in the feral plains of an ex-mining village, Newstead, Nottinghamshire. In the shadow of Lord Byron's grandeur, he was part of an existence that was (and is) ignored by the media. Editor and co-founder of Hi Vis Press, he tries to encourage the lesser voiced truths of our society. *The Bygones* is his first full length collection.

October 2022

This first edition is published
as a trade paperback; there are 126 numbered &
lettered copies signed by the author, & handbound
in boards by the Tangerine Press, Tooting, London;
lettered copies also contain signed
artwork by Julia Soboleva.